Flooded

A Story about a Storm (and Robots!)

Thunderchickens Robotics (# 217)

Written By: *Sitara Murali, Christina Li, Manvir Sandhu, Jason Li, Nygel Sejismundo, Kevin Li, Cameron Gudobba*

Illustrated By: *Christina Li, Hannah Imboden*

TABLE OF CONTENTS

DEDICATION

~~~

We would like to dedicate this book to all the teachers who have inspired creative and innovative minds.

Prologue

Aaronville was a quiet little town on the slope of a valley just a few miles away from the ocean. Its happy citizens went about their days greeting neighbors, running errands, and maybe stopping for a sandwich at the local deli. The kids went to school, the parents went to work, and the elderly sat out on their rocking chairs, smiling and waving at the people passing by. Truly, the most remarkable thing about Aaronville was how *little* seemed to happen there. A pie-eating contest took place every autumn and the annual spelling bee in the spring, but that was about as much excitement as you could find. The people of Aaronville were as content as could be with their peaceful lives and simple routines.

Unfortunately for them, however, something drastic was about to happen.

It began as a regular summer Wednesday with a gentle breeze rolling in from the ocean and the sun shining down on the little town. The weatherman on the local news station had warned of an approaching severe storm the day before, but no one had paid any attention. The people went about their lives just as they always did, with the kids playing happily outside and the adults working dutifully [1] away. It wasn't until minutes after noon that black rainclouds started rolling across the sky. They were like giant, gray monsters hanging over the town, ready to shower it with a storm more terrible than anyone could remember. Water droplets fell from the sky, and they just didn't stop.

It poured ...

and it poured ...

and then it poured some more.

By night, the storm had only gotten worse. There was thunder so loud and lightning so bright that it shook and lit up the entire town. No one in Aaronville slept soundly that night. Buckets upon buckets of water swept over the town, and gusts of wind added to the devastation. The water flowed until the whole valley of Aaronville was completely flooded.

---

[1] doing something you are expected to

By next morning, the storm had stopped just as suddenly as it had started. Although the storm was over, it left behind a trail of ruin: fallen trees, power out, crushed cars and blocked roads. Worst of all, the town's system of pumps for maintaining the flow of water was broken. All of the once-happy people of Aaronville woke up to find that most of their quiet little town in its quiet little valley was under four feet of water.

Chapter 1
KELLY

Kelly's House, Morning after the Storm

Someone was shaking me awake, but I was too comfortable in my cocoon of blankets to care.

"Mmph," I groaned.

"Kelly!" The voice was urgent.

"Wha-?" I yawned and blinked open my eyes. My mom was sitting on the side of my bed, looking worried. I checked the time. 7:45 a.m. ... on a Saturday? My family always slept in on Saturdays. Something wasn't right.

"Mom, is everything okay?" I asked. "What's going on?"

"The storm last night caused major flooding," Mom answered. "Everything in the valley is completely under water."

I shot up, startled by the news.

"But if it's flooded, why are we still at home?" I asked. "Shouldn't we have been evacuated or something? Is it even safe to be here?" My mind was filled with a flurry of questions.

"Well, the flood didn't affect our part of town too much," she answered. That made sense. Our neighborhood was on much higher ground.

"But, our basement is pretty damaged. And a lot of people in the valley did have to be evacuated from their homes, including Maiya's family."

My heart sank; Maiya was my best friend and she was like a sister to me.

Both of our moms had grown up in Aaronville, so Maiya and I were practically destined to be best friends. You wouldn't have guessed it by looking at us, though: she has dark brown hair, I have blonde; she's tall, I'm short; she has a huge family, my family is just my mom and me. However, I'm glad we're different because it is what made us so close.

"Is everyone okay?" I asked frantically[2].

"Yes, yes, everyone in her family is fine," my mom reassured me. "A little shaken up, but fine. I told them to stay at our place for now. They're all downstairs."

I breathed a sigh of relief. They were like my second family. "Well, what's gonna happen now?"

"Actually, that's why I woke you up," said my mom. "The mayor

---

[2] in a panic

announced that she's holding a meeting to discuss where to go from here."

"Wait, how did you find out?" I asked. "I thought the power was out."

"The mayor spoke on a radio broadcast," said my mom. "But, sweetie, you need to get ready so we can all head over."

"Okay," I nodded. She hugged me tightly and left the room. We both knew how lucky we were to be safe.

~~~

I got ready in eight minutes, a personal record. I rushed downstairs to overhear our two families talking anxiously about the town meeting. Maiya and I ran up to each other, feeling extremely relieved to see each other safe.

Everyone hurriedly gulped [3] down their food. We all wanted to get to the

---

[3] to eat quickly

meeting at Abbott Elementary School as soon as possible. Fortunately, the building was on high ground and wasn't damaged by the storm, so we could drive to it.

Bad storms aren't uncommon. There were fallen trees from the lightning, as expected, but I had never seen the roads like this. It was like being in a very large and muddy kiddie pool. Maiya's dad told me that all the businesses in the valley were closed. Up here, there were sandbags all along the street, but they didn't seem to be helping much. Workers from the electric company were everywhere, trying to repair the power lines that had fallen. Police cars were parked every which way, and an officer walked over to our stopped minivan. My mom rolled the driver's window down.

"Hello, officer," she said.

"Good morning, ma'am," the officer

replied. "Are you all headed to the meeting?" He yawned, clearly exhausted.

"Yes, sir."

"You're going to have to park in this temporary lot and take the bus," he said.

I saw a couple of my school friends on the bus with their families, but they all just sort of smiled at me and looked away. No one on the bus spoke. I hated it. I wanted to get up and tell everyone that things were going to be okay, that we should all stop acting so sad, but I knew that would be insensitive. Some of these people had lost their homes and businesses.

When we got off of the bus, things weren't looking much better. There was a huge crowd but everyone was still quiet. We were trying to make sense of the mess around us. Before long, Mayor Arscheene walked up to the podium.

"Good morning, citizens," she announced. "Yesterday was a hard day for all of us. As you know, there was a severe storm last night, and it was worse than we expected. The unexpected amount of water has caused extreme flooding in our city, mainly in the valley. The pump systems below our streets that usually filter out water have been overwhelmed by the thunderstorm. There are too many leaks, and even though we were able to determine where they are, it's too dangerous to fix the pumps directly due to possible electrocution[4].

"I have come up with a short-term plan for keeping the city safe. All businesses and schools will be closed for at least 48 hours. Aaronville Hospital has already been shut down. The patients have been relocated, and

---

[4] to injure by electricity

those in critical condition were airlifted to a safer place. In addition, following this meeting, our police and fire departments can relocate anyone who needs a temporary place to stay to Abbott Elementary. We have already evacuated many families from the valley to Abbott Elementary. As for transportation, please keep driving to a minimum. The buses are doing their best to be available at all times. In this time of need, we are asking you all to help fix this city. Therefore, we will soon host another meeting to gather ideas on how exactly to go about mending our lives.

"Be strong and don't give up hope because, together, we will find a way to come back from this. Every single one of you is encouraged to help out. You may think your idea is impossible, but you can save your neighbors, your community, and your city just by sharing. You can help."

Chapter 2
MIKE

Mike's Mechanic Shop, Before the Town Meeting

I'd seen some nasty things happen in my day but the flood was unlike anything I've ever witnessed.

So much of our fair city was ruined: the bakery, the grocery store, the gas station, even the ice cream parlor. Almost every business and many homes had taken some very serious damage. The people hurt in the storm had to be taken to the next town over because Aaronville Hospital was uninhabitable[5]. Everyone seemed to have an air of despair[6] about them as they made their way out of their damaged homes. What about me, you ask? Well, I was one of the lucky ones. Mike's Mechanic Shop is on the far edge of town on a bit of a hill, sparing[7] it from the serious flooding from which other businesses had suffered.

I made my way down to Abbott Elementary School. Most of Aaronville's citizens were already clustered[8] there like sardines in a can (which I suppose is fitting considering all of the water around them). Even though Mayor Arscheene gave her

---

[5] unable to be lived in

[6] gloomy or sad environment

[7] to hold back from harming or destroying

[8] standing close together

speech about how everyone can help, you could tell only a few of us believed it.

As people filed out, the desperate looks on their faces told me they were overwhelmed. Everyone was afraid. Afraid of the water surrounding them, and especially afraid of the fact that their lives had been so severely changed.

Only a handful of us remained after everyone left. There were just a few people who had gone up to the podium to get more information. It was no surprise that most of whom were left had careers and skills that might be useful. What surprised me was that a little girl and her friend had stayed behind. They couldn't have been more than 11 or 12 years old. The girl with blonde hair looked familiar though. I think she won the spelling bee once. Kathy? No. Kelly? Yeah, Kelly sounds right. Anyway, we all gathered around the mayor's podium to discuss how to take care of the flooding.

"What specifically is wrong with the pumps?" I asked Mayor Arscheene. I don't remember much of what the mayor had to say because it didn't really matter to me. I already had my idea, and I knew that it would solve our problem: I'm going to build a robot to patch up the pumps. I'd been thinking about it for most of the morning, and I knew I could finish it quickly.

So really, it didn't matter what the others had to say. I dismissed Kelly's idea that we could all work together because people have different skills. It just doesn't work that way. I mean, she was trying to help. It's not her fault that her idea was just not possible.

Chapter 3
MAIYA

Abbott Elementary School, After the Town Meeting

"Maiya, sweetie, hold my hand, okay? Be careful in the streets. I don't want to lose you in this chaos," my mom said, looking at me with worry.

"Mom, I'll be fine."

"Just be careful."

"I will, but, Mom, do we have to go back on the bus right now? Kelly and I want to stay and help."

"Oh, I don't know about that, dear.

It's not very safe," my mom said, as she pulled me close.

"Pleeeeease, Mom? Kelly's mom is staying with her. I'll stay with them and come back super fast."

I could tell that my mom was giving in, but she gave me another concerned look before taking me to Kelly and her mom. Kelly and I had been separated during the confusion of the meeting, but one look at her face and I knew that the same thoughts were running through our heads.

"Hi," I whispered to her, giving her a hug.

"Hey, you," Kelly said, her forehead wrinkling in concentration.

"What are you thinking about?" I asked her.

"Do you believe what the mayor said? That just one person's idea can save the town?"

"No, I don't. But, someone has to try, right?"

"And that someone could be us!" Kelly exclaimed, passionately.

"Us? What in the world can we do?" I said, unconvinced.

"Hey! Don't have that kind of attitude! We've got to be able to help in some way."

We quickly made our way to the mayor's podium.

~~~

After Mr. Mike asked his questions, Mayor Arscheene told us what was needed to fix the broken pumps. Too much water had caused holes in the old, rusted pumps, so the mayor told us the exact location of the leaks in the pipeworks. There weren't many people listening to the mayor's explanation, just the few that had stayed behind. Almost everyone looked at us with annoyance, either wondering why we were there or wishing we weren't. How were we supposed to help if no one thought we could?

I could tell that Kelly and I were having the same doubts, but one of us had to be strong. "Come on, Kelly. You were the one who told me that we can help somehow! Let's not quit now. Why don't we ask Mayor Arscheene if we can help in any way?" I asked her, trying to make the best of this.

Kelly brightened up, "Okay, Maiya, that's a good idea. Let's go catch up to the mayor before she leaves!"

Kelly's mom had stayed close to us, and after Mayor Arscheene's response, she whispered, "Kelly, Maiya, maybe we should just head home now."

"Mom, we have to help! Pleeeeease?" Kelly whined, putting on her best puppy dog face.

Finally, Kelly's mom gave in, and I spoke up. "Excuse me, Mayor Arscheene?" I asked, nervously.

She turned to face Kelly and me, but the look on her face said she just saw two little kids. Clearly, she didn't think much of us. "Hi, kids. How can I help you two?"

"Well, we were actually wondering how we could help ... with the flood. Is there anything we can do?" I said as confidently as I could.

"Oh, don't you kids worry about this."

Kelly frowned and looked at me. I nudged [9] her, wanting her to say something.

"Ma'am, we are worried. And we'd like to help."

"Hmm, well, there are a lot of people going through a tough time. The police and fire departments are guiding the people who were hit the hardest to the auditorium, so why don't you young ladies go over there and help them out?" Mayor Arscheene suggested.

"Oh. Well, I mean I guess we could,"

---

[9] to push gently to get someone's attention

I said, sadly. Kelly and I looked at each other, feeling discouraged. "Mom, can we go to the auditorium and visit with the people who have to stay there?"

"Sure, sweetie," she agreed.

I was surprised by her response, but I guess the auditorium was the safest place to be right then. We made our way there, disappointed with by the busy work we had been assigned.

Chapter 4
XANDER

Xander's House, During the Town Meeting

I sat on the couch, staring at my window. I could hardly believe what happened. Thoughts were racing through my mind as I watched the helpless looks on people's faces while they struggled through the water. I thought about the amount of damage that this flood caused, but brainstorming ideas about what I could do to help was difficult. As a high school student, there was only so much that I could do, so I was hoping that Mayor Arscheene would think of a solution quickly. My parents had gone out of town to visit my grandparents, and I was home alone. After 17 years, they finally trusted me to stay home by myself, but now, thanks to this flood, I would never get to stay home by myself again. There's no point to even go to this meeting since my parents are fine, and I'm fine. I mean, all I would do at the meeting is joke around and try to lighten the mood, but I'm sure the townspeople would not be appreciative[10] of that.

But then again ... even if my biggest talent is making jokes, I always found the idea of electricity to be interesting.

---

[10] feeling grateful

So the question now is how can a high school student messing with electricity save a town? I'm great at working with wires and batteries but not tools. A while back, I asked Mike if I could be his apprentice just to have something to do. But on the first day of my apprenticeship [11], I was carelessly mixing his system with my wires and accidentally took out his power. After that mess, he dismissed me. Mike didn't think I was taking it seriously enough, so I could understand why he did it. But, it was the first day. He could've given me a warning or something.

Back to the issue at hand. The more I thought about what I could do to help, the more I realized how much I could actually do; electricity doesn't play well with water, but if there is a

---

[11] a person who works for another in order to learn a certain skill

way to insulate the electricity cheaply, then I may have just figured out a way to help.

To give my mind a break, I decided to go outside. I opened the door slowly, and the damage I observed outside grew and grew with each inch. The destruction was a lot worse than I had expected.

I stood there for a moment to just take it all in: the fallen trees, the cars stuck in the water, and even a man helping someone get out of his car through the sunroof. I looked down and saw that the flowers and bushes on both sides of my front steps were consumed by the water.

"At least I know I won't need to water them for a while," I joked, trying to make myself feel better. I sat down on the steps of my porch and dipped my feet in the mud, then stretched my arms back behind me and set them on the ground. I was trying to stay relaxed, but it wasn't working.

Everyone looked so sad, and it made sense. Their lives were greatly impacted by this flood, even if mine wasn't. I could tell that I was one of the lucky ones because my house was on high ground. But, I had this feeling inside me— like when I see my friend getting hurt, or someone getting made fun of. It was the feeling of empathy [12] and wanting to help. I realized that sitting back doing nothing was not the right thing to do. I needed to do something right away.

Looking at the downed power lines on the street, I suddenly remembered one of my old side projects I had abandoned: waterproof wire connectors. Technically, all wires with plastic casing around are waterproof,

---

[12] being able to relate to how someone feels or thinks

but electrocution happens when there are breaks in the casing, specifically with the junctions[13]. In fact, I think they are still downstairs in my basement! I leapt up, ran back inside my house and straight to the den. I had started it as part of a device that shampooed my hair and brushed my teeth for me.

But now, with this disaster, my wires could be an important part in solving this problem. My toothbrush could wait. If I can just figure out a way to waterproof some wires fully, then we can replace any old electrical system with one that would actually work in the water.

---

[13] a point where two or more things are joined

Chapter 5
RUCHI

Coffee Shop, 4:00 p.m.

I was sitting in my favorite coffee shop in my usual spot when a voice suddenly asked me, "Why are you here by yourself?" I looked up, startled, and saw a pair of young girls standing next to me. I needed some place quiet to work if I wanted to save the town, and I wasn't expecting company.

"Um ... hi? I'm by myself because it's easier to think and program when

I'm alone. When there are a lot of people, I can't get any work done."

"I'm Kelly, and this is Maiya," the blonde one piped up. "What's your name? What does 'program' mean?"

"I'm Ruchi. Programming [14] means to write instructions to a computer and get it to do something, usually by reading information from sensors. The code is the instruction."

Kelly looked over to the notepad where I was scribbling my ideas. "This looks complicated."

"And this isn't even code!" I smiled. "This is pseudocode [15] . It's just simplified code without the computer language written in."

"Oh, so pseudocode is the basic

---

[14] process of typing instructions in a special language so the computer can understand them

[15] an outline of the code to make it easier to write

version of what you want to translate?"

"Yep!"

"Why are you writing pseudocode?" Maiya added.

"I'm a programmer, and I want to use my skills to help the town remove the flood water from the thunderstorm. I know the pumps are damaged, so right now, I'm trying to program the pumps to shut off the branches that have leaks. But I don't know how we can even put that into action since I'm not sure if the pumps have been computerized."

Kelly nodded, deep in thought. Then she said, "Why don't you work with other people? I promise they won't be a distraction."

I sighed. "It's not that they're a distraction, Kelly, it's just that they don't understand me. It gets kind of lonely when you're speaking a language that they don't get." This was also part of the reason why I liked to work alone, sitting in a coffee shop instead of in an office or a meeting room.

"I understand," Kelly said. "But I can help!"

"How?"

"I heard Mike saying at the meeting that he was making a robot to fix the pumps. Do you think you can write pseudocode to make the robot come to life?" Kelly asked.

I wrinkled my forehead. "Yeah, it shouldn't be too hard. But I don't think he'd want me there. I'm only a high school student."

Kelly shook her head. "And I'm only ten, but I'll get it to work out somehow. Tell me when you finish your pseudocode, okay? When you are ready to code everything, the robot will be completely finished and waiting for your finishing touches. I promise."

That did seem to be a good idea. It would certainly save me the trouble of computerizing the pumps. "Okay. You do that. The pseudocode isn't going to take much longer. And I'd love to work on robotics!"

"Thanks, Ruchi!" Maiya said. She and Kelly walked away, looking happy. I smiled, thinking that with their help and leadership, we could really save the town. Together.

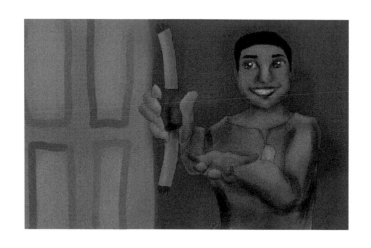

Chapter 6
XANDER

Xander's House, 4:30 p.m.

Just when I began connecting one of the junctions to some wires, the doorbell upstairs rang. I quickly bounded [16] upstairs and opened the door. It turned out to be my neighbor, Kelly, and her friend, Maiya.

"Hi girls! What's up?" I said.

Kelly smiled brightly at me. "Hi,

---

[16] run with big strides

Xander! I was just wondering if you needed help with anything since I know your parents are out of town. Are you okay?"

I laughed. "I'll probably be grounded for years because my parents will somehow find a way to blame me for the flooding, but I'm fine! I'm actually working on some waterproof connectors to help with this problem."

Maiya looked at me quizzically. "Connectors to what?" she asked.

I grabbed one of my connectors out of my pocket that I had finished earlier. "Connectors to other wires. The parts of an electrical system that get destroyed with water are usually at the links of wires because the copper ends of the wires are open to the water. The plastic casing of the wire is fine if water hits it, but the copper isn't. I waterproofed the copper by covering the exposed parts with a material called potting that doesn't conduct [17] electricity," I explained. "Then I covered the potting with another substance called mould [18] , which is the blue part you see here. It's smooth so even when water hits the potting, it would slide right over instead of going into tiny cracks."

Kelly looked thoughtful. "I get it! So you're basically just making all the wires one giant connected wire so no water can get through, right?"

I nodded happily. "Yup, and I just got it to work. I don't know exactly where to put these connectors yet, but it's still early. After the water goes away in a few days, then I'll figure something out." I noticed their bikes lying scattered on my lawn. "What are you girls up to?" I asked.

---

[17] to allow electricity to pass through it

[18] a waterproof substance

"We're just helping anyone who needs anything. After we begged her, my mom let us go around the safe parts of town to talk to people. A lot of people have been displaced [19] from their homes because of the floodwaters, so mostly, we've just been grabbing valuable items for our neighbors and bringing them to the families at Abbott Elementary. We've helped ten people so far," Kelly said proudly. But then she frowned a little. "I wish we could help out even more though. We're making an impact, but there are so many people who won't be able to return home because the pumps aren't working, and the streets are still flooded."

"Maybe you can use my idea somehow," I added. "Everything will work out eventually. Even if it means

---

[19] moved or put out of the usual or proper place

an entire crew of people mopping up the water on the street, droplet by droplet, we'll figure it out," I joked.

"We'll keep asking around to see if anyone needs help then. It was great talking to you, Xander!" The two girls gave me a hug and ran off to their bikes, waving good bye as they went.

Grinning, I closed my door and returned downstairs to perfect my connectors.

Chapter 7
MIKE

Mike's Mechanic Shop, 5:00 p.m.

"Darn it!" I yelled in frustration.

The robot was running into a few problems. Oh, who was I kidding? Everything that could possibly go wrong with this robot was going wrong. Not mechanically. I mean, mechanics are the one thing I know best. If you asked me to build you a bicycle out of scrap metal or make a

41

toaster to replace the one you broke, I could do it in an instant. But once I was out of the building stage, my other problems came up.

My first version of the robot had two claws to patch up the pump leaks, a compartment on its back to hold the patches, and two traction[20] wheels to push through bumpy terrain, like mini Jeep wheels.

The biggest problem was the wiring. Every time I pushed my robot around for a trial run, its wires sparked and the lights fizzed out whenever the robot touched the puddles of water on the ground. How am I going to get this thing to fix the pumps, which are underwater?

To add to my ever-growing pile of confusing problems, I couldn't seem to make the robot do what I wanted it to do. Right now, the robot runs when I

---

[20] ability for an object to grab onto a surface

wind it up. It goes forward to where a pump would be, grabs a patch from its compartment, and then attaches it to the leak so it'll be closed. But unless I place the robot in the perfect position directly in front of the leak, it would fix up the wrong area because it can't sense where it should put the patch. And even with the sensors I have, how can I communicate the information from the sensors to the robot's movements?

While I grumbled about this stupid robot, the girls from the meeting walked into my shop.

"Hi Mr. Mike," the blonde one exclaimed, annoyingly cheery. "I'm Kelly, and I want to help out! How is your little robot looking?"

"Little robot?" I shoot back. "I'll have you know, young lady, the fate of the entire city rests on the back of my 'little robot.' It'd do you good to treat it with some respect!"

"Oh, I'm sorry," Kelly answered, not sounding apologetic at all. "Is there anything Maiya and I can do to help though?"

I glanced at her, almost amused. "Well, what do you two know about mechanical and electrical engineering?"

Kelly's face falls. "Nothing really," she answered in a quiet voice.

"Well then, how do you expect to help me in any way?" I shot back.

"Umm," Kelly thinks for a moment. "What problems are you having?"

"What problems am I not having would be a better question," I snapped back. "There is water everywhere, and this is an electrically-powered robot. I can't get it to read information from the sensors. I'm sure you can see the issue. Even if I could solve that problem, I don't know how to make the darn thing do what I want it to do and go where I want it to go!"

"Oh!" Kelly exclaimed. "There's a boy named Xander that lives in my neighborhood who's really good with wires and stuff! And there's a girl I just talked to, Ruchi, who's great with programming! Why don't you ask them to help you?"

"No!" I immediately responded. "That Xander kid has never cared about anything. I tried to take him on as an apprentice once. On the first day, he cut off the power to my shop because he was messing around. And I've never heard Ruchi say a single word to anyone. No, I don't need any help. I can do this all on my own."

Kelly looked defeated. "Well, alright, Mr. Mike. Sorry for bothering you. We'll be going now."

I watched them walk away. I know they had good intentions and I probably could have been a little nicer, but this was not the time for kids and their silly ideas. I went back to my robot and wound it up, but it immediately drove straight out of the shop and into the puddles of water.

"Darn it!" I exclaimed.

Chapter 8
KELLY

Biking Home, 6:00 p.m.

"Hey, you okay?" Maiya asked from a few feet behind me. We were biking home after checking in with everyone, and she probably felt my frustration after our conversation with Mr. Mike.

I pursed my lips and tried to gather myself. I was so lost in my thoughts that I didn't respond for a few minutes. Maiya was still waiting for a response, so I knew I had to answer her one way or another.

"I know Mr. Mike was under a lot of stress. I mean, building a robot is hard enough without a time limit on it. But he didn't have to be so rude to us," I answered.

"I know, right?" exclaimed Maiya. "But don't take it too personally. He was just taking out his frustration on you. We came at the wrong time. He clearly was having issues with his robot thingy."

Part of me wanted to think Maiya was right. She was the wisest 6th grader I knew, and she always knew the right thing to say. But she wasn't seeing the whole picture this time. I wasn't upset just because of Mr. Mike's comments. Usually, comments like his rolled right off my back. It wasn't his comments that were bothering me; it was the tone of voice he used.

He talked to me like I was

incapable[21] of doing anything. As if I was just an innocent four-year-old who doesn't know right from left. Well, I do! I know lots of things. I know wheels need something to rotate around; I know there is no pot of gold at the end of a rainbow; I know my multiplication tables up to 14, and I know that the only way Aaronville will get out of this mess is if we work together.

I really wish the adults in this town would stop treating Maiya and me like small children. Even Mayor Arscheene was doing it! She gave us that job to "spread the word" just to get rid of us. I could totally tell because she was using that voice adults use when they talk to little kids. That baby, cootchie-coo voice that drives me absolutely bonkers!

I guess Maiya sensed my irritation

---

[21] not able

because she asked, "Dude, seriously, what is wrong?"

"It's just … don't you feel like the adults around here treat us sort of like little kids?"

Maiya sighed. "Yeah, I noticed it, too. It seems to be seriously bothering you, though."

"Well, yeah, of course it bothers me! I mean, not to toot my own horn or anything, but I get pretty good grades in school and I won the spelling bee this year and … I'm intelligent … okay! And for that matter, so are you! Why do they treat us like we're completely dense?"

Maiya looked alarmed. I was always the calm, cool, and collected one. I never lost my temper like that. But this time, I was seriously upset, and I had to let it out.

"Do you think I am completely stupid?" I whispered. "I mean, maybe I've been fooling myself. Maybe grades don't really mean much in the grand scheme of things. And anyone can win an old spelling bee. I guess I don't really know much about robots and wires and code and all of that. Maybe the adults are right; I shouldn't stick my nose in this. They know what to do. I'm just a kid."

I looked at Maiya. She opened her mouth to say something, then closed it and looked away.

"We should really get back," she said softly. We rode the rest of the way home in silence.

Chapter 9
MAIYA

Kelly's House, 6:30 p.m.

Hearing Kelly talk about herself like that made me feel so sad and helpless. What could I say to convince her that she was one of the smartest, probably the smartest friend I have? When we got to her house, she just walked up to the sofa and lied down, looking defeated. I searched my mind, thinking of anything I could say to show her how inspirational she really could be. Then it suddenly came to me. It was obvious.

"Hey, Kelly, listen to me for a second." She turned to me, a sad look on her face, and I walked over to sit on the arm of the sofa. "I totally think you can bring everyone together. After all, you've done it before!"

"What are you talking about?" she asked, looking confused.

"Well, don't you remember that big group project that we had last year? Two days before we had to turn in our diorama of The Louvre Museum[22] and give our presentation, Katrina's little brother pushed the whole model off his dining table. Our entire project was ruined, and Mr. Moraccini wasn't very understanding. But, guess who fixed it?" I asked enthusiastically[23].

---

[22] one of the world's largest museums, located in Paris, France

[23] feeling eager or excited

Kelly smiled a little, remembering what had happened.

"You!" I shouted happily. "Kelly, that was all you. We would have failed if you hadn't explained how each group member could use their own talents to recreate the project. You told Katrina and Grace how they could work on what was left of the diorama and reconstruct it because they had been so good at that in the first place. And then you showed me that I had the ability to edit the presentation to fit the new diagram, and in the end, we finished on time and with a great grade."

"Thank you, Maiya, but I don't see why that relates to this issue."

"Come on, Kelly. For someone so smart, you can be a little clueless sometimes," I joked.

She gave me a silly look, so I continued, "Kelly, you know the talents of everyone in town! Mike with his robot that doesn't work right, Xander with his waterproof wires, and Ruchi with her pseudocode. We just checked in with everybody, and I know that if you just bring them together physically to one place, then it will all work out! Maybe when they actually see how all their parts can fit together, then we can save the town."

Kelly stopped looking so sad and started to brighten up. "You know what, Maiya, maybe you're right. I knew there was a reason we were best friends," she said, pulling me into a hug.

I laughed, hugging her back, and we started to plan our speech to bring everyone together.

~~~

"Okay, let's do this," Kelly whispered once she got her mother's attention. "Hey, Mom? Can we run an idea by you for how to fix the town?"

"Sure, girls. What do you have in

mind?"

"Okay, so Mike has a robot. It doesn't work because he can't get the wires to work near so much water, but Xander, our neighbor, made waterproof wiring!" Kelly explained.

"Wasn't there some trouble with Mike and Xander a while ago? Are you sure they'll want to work together?" Kelly's mom questioned.

"Well, they'll have to if it determines the fate of our town," I countered[24]. "And if we announce it at the next town meeting with everyone's attention on them, Mike probably won't be able to say no."

"All right, what's next?" Kelly said, but she didn't pause or give me time to answer before she continued. "The robot Mike's creating doesn't seem to do what he wants. But, today, when we met Ruchi, she explained how code

___

[24] respond against a belief

can tell the robot exactly what to do by reading information from its sensors. And if Mike and Xander can get past their differences, then Ruchi can program a solution to make the robot actually do things!"

"That's right. And at the next meeting, we're going to wait to see if Mayor Arscheene has any new information, and then we're going to explain to everyone how they can work together," I said, feeling triumphant[25] about our plan.

Kelly's mom clapped for our idea. "I'm impressed! You did an amazing job with gathering information. Here's some more good news: Mayor Arscheene announced about an hour ago that there'll be another town meeting tomorrow morning. She said she wants everybody's ideas ready by then, and anyone with something to

---

[25] successful

say is welcome to come. You guys have a brilliant plan ready, so I think you can really help save us all!"

But suddenly, Kelly looked worried again. "What if they don't listen to us?"

"Hey, they have to be considerate[26] enough to listen to us, and our plan is awesome!" I reassured Kelly. "Even if they don't like the fact that we're kids, they'll put aside our age because working together will actually fix our town."

"You're right, Maiya."

"Kelly, it was all your idea! You got this!"

"No, Maiya, it was both of ours. I couldn't have done it if you didn't convince me I could."

---

[26] showing care for another's feelings

Chapter 10
KELLY

Abbott Elementary, Second Town Meeting

My mom drove us to the town meeting with Maiya's parents the next morning. They were pretty annoyed that Maiya and I had been, according to them, "gallivanting[27] around town during an emergency situation" without letting them know where we

---

[27] to wander around

were. When they stopped yelling long enough to let us get a word in, we explained that we were trying to help the town. Plus, the mayor gave us an important job to do. We described everything we did the day before to Maiya's parents to catch them up.

The parents cooled off a little bit after that, but we could tell we weren't off the hook yet for not telling them. I'm just glad they let us go to the meeting. Maiya and I had come up with the perfect plan, and I would be seriously upset if we weren't able to present it to the town.

The entire way there, I was whispering the whole thing to myself over and over again so I wouldn't forget. I mean, it's not like I have a bad memory or anything. I just... don't do very well under pressure. School reports weren't a big deal because I knew that stuff inside out and backwards. Plus, those presentations were always in front of my classmates. It was way more pressure to present to the mayor, the Aaronville City Council, and a dozen adults who think I have no business being there.

Yeah. Way more pressure.

While I was freaking out, Maiya was silently staring out the window. Her face was blank, but I knew, deep down, she was as anxious as I was. She was trying to keep it together for my sake. That's one of the best things about her. She may not know a lot about pseudocode or waterproof wires, but she knows a lot about people. And she knew one of us needed to stay sane if we were going to actually do this.

Our parents looked a little bit nervous, but it wasn't just because we told them about our idea. We also told them how we wanted to be a part of the town's decisions. I had said,

"Maiya and I will become voting citizens in a few years. If we don't know the first thing about our city's government, how will we ever make the right decisions about it?"

They were pretty surprised by that. I guess they didn't realize how often Maiya and I actually listen to the news.

By the time we reached the bus parking lot for people going to Abbott Elementary, I had repeated the plan approximately thirty-four times. There was no way I could mess it up unless I froze. But with Maiya by my side, I knew it would all work out. She would never let that happen.

After the short bus ride, we walked into the auditorium the city had set up for the meeting. It was a lot more organized than the first meeting was, probably because they had more time to plan it. There were six rows of tables spanning the large width of the room, with chairs tucked neatly under them. A solid 120 people or so could fit in there snugly, and they did.

Maiya and I stared at each other in disbelief. We were working under the impression that only a handful of people would be there, like last time. Instead, it looked like half the town had shown up!

We picked seats near the front as part of our plan. That way, we wouldn't lose our cool when everyone turned around to look at us when we raised our hands. Our parents sat one row behind us.

Maiya took my hand and squeezed it quickly before she let go. She looked at me with so much confidence, I couldn't help but smile back. I opened my mouth to say something to her, but before I could, the mayor and city council walked in briskly[28].

---

[28] fast and energetically

"Hello, ladies and gentlemen!" said Mayor Arscheene. "I am so happy to see you all here today. As you can see, some of the flooding has been kept under control with help from the Aaronville Fire and Police Departments. I would like to take a moment to thank all of our emergency workers for their service over the past couple of days. Without their hustle, the situation could have gotten a lot worse a lot quicker."

Mayor Arscheene had to stop speaking when the entire room erupted[29] in applause.

"Like I said, some of the flooding has been kept under control," she continued. "But, there is still a lot of water left. With this meeting, I hope to find a solution that will get rid of the water, and quickly. That's where you all, the citizens of Aaronville,

---

[29] to break out dramatically

come in.

"To suggest an idea, all you have to do is grab a slip of paper and pen from the basket that's coming around and write your idea down. Then we'll gather them together to pick the best one."

When the slips came to Maiya, she wrote our idea to combine Mike's robot, Xander's wires, and Ruchi's programming.

After everyone passed their ideas back in, Mayor Arscheene announced, "Thank you very much. Now, we will randomly pick one person at a time. We'd like to get to everyone's ideas quickly, so keep your presentations short. We have about thirty ideas to introduce."

That was really surprising. I imagined that some of the people here were like our moms— they just came to hear the ideas, not present any. That's what Maiya and I were supposed to be doing, but we were tired of staying silent.

"I will treat everyone's ideas with the same amount of respect," continued Mayor Arscheene. "I expect the same courtesy to be extended to everyone here."

The presentations started right away. Some of them were pretty crazy. For example, someone wanted to move the city on rocket boosters and just leave the water here. Mr. Mike presented his robot to patch up the pumps, which was the only concrete solution we had seen so far. He had made a fake broken pump and put it the table for the robot to fix, but based on what we saw, the robot wasn't good enough. The robot missed patching the right part of the pipe more times than it actually did it right, even when Mr. Mike positioned it himself. How would it work underwater, where he can't put it in the exact position?

Xander followed Mr. Mike with his own presentation of his waterproof wires. "Here are just two normal wires," he introduced, holding each end of the wire from a light bulb in his hand and pointing out the open copper. "Normally, if the copper is exposed underwater, it can electrocute people. But ...," he paused.

He quickly snapped a small connector so his invention covered the copper, then dropped the ends into a glass of water. The bulb lit up brightly, and everyone gasped when he touched the wire to prove it wouldn't short out or shock anyone. "Don't be too *shocked*," Xander joked.

Once everyone had gotten over their excitement over Xander's wire, the mayor picked the next-to-last slip. It wasn't Maiya and me, but we knew we had to be the last ones. Great. Mrs. Hobble, who lives two blocks away with six cats, gave her idea of bringing in a thousand dogs to lap away all the water. We all clapped politely, and Maiya and I looked at each other. We could totally do this. They clearly saved the best for last. Plus, after hearing everyone's plans, we could weave [30] them all together much better.

"Maiya and Kelly," said Mayor Arscheene. I might have just been seeing things, but she looked surprised. What I definitely saw was my mom exchanging a look with Maiya's mom.

Maiya and I made our way to the podium. I stopped once I saw all the people staring at me, but Maiya pushed me to the microphone when she sensed my hesitation. I cleared my throat and started.

"Hello, everyone. My name is Kelly

---

[30] to combine various elements to make a new whole

and this is my best friend, Maiya. We're in the sixth grade. A lot of people think that means we don't know much about, well, anything really. But, honestly, we do. We spent the better part of yesterday checking with everyone as they tried to work on their solutions. And, with all due respect, we realized the adults missed something. Big."

The crowd started buzzing with whispers, but Mayor Arscheene quickly shushed them.

I quickly continued, "No single person in this room can fix our town. Not alone, at least. Mr. Mike, you're really on to something with your robot. I'm not going to lie, Maiya and I aren't completely sure what you want to accomplish with it since you won't be there to move it in the right place. But it won't work if you don't ask other people for help.

"Your robot isn't working because

none of its parts can communicate with each other. The sensors won't work, and the wires would short once it's in water. Xander is onto something with his wires. He can help you waterproof your wires so they won't break underwater. And Ruchi is an amazing programmer. She can help the robot use its sensors with code so you won't have to position it yourself to fix the pumps."

"Mr. Mike," added Maiya. "You are really, really good at what you do. And so are Xander and Ruchi. Everyone in this town has talents and skills, and if we want to fix Aaronville, we have to make sure we use them to our advantage. We have to work together. And that doesn't just mean everyone working directly on the robot. It means using everyone's ideas. We heard some pretty good ones today."

"Here's what we have, and we're confident about it. Mayor Arscheene, we hope you will approve our solution," I finished.

Everyone was quietly staring at us. It was pretty frightening. But I took a deep breath and followed Maiya off the stage anyway. That was scary, but I'm glad we did it.

"Well," said Mayor Arscheene. "Maiya and Kelly sure gave us all a lot to think about. Please give the council and me a few minutes to discuss our decision. We will let you know soon."

Our moms looked like they were on the verge [31] of tears. Maiya and I looked at each other for the hundredth time that day, this time in confusion.

"Are you guys okay?" asked Maiya.

"Yes, we just ...," said Maiya's mom. "We're so proud of you both, getting up there like that." She pulled my mom, Maiya, and me into a very cramped, tearful group hug. The tears

---

[31] to be close to

were from the moms.

"Okay, ladies and gentlemen," said Mayor Arscheene. That was quick. "The council and I have made a decision. We agree with Maiya and Kelly. The only way to clean up Aaronville is to have a team made up of the best and the brightest. The team we have assembled consists of Mr. Mike, Xander, Ruchi, Maiya, and Kelly. We expect that you will meet as soon as possible. I will be at Mike's garage later to see how far you have come. I don't need to remind this team how important it is for them to work quickly and efficiently[32]. Aaronville is counting on you."

Well, jeez. No pressure or anything.

---

[32] working in the best way possible, using the least time and effort

Chapter 11
MIKE

Mike's Mechanic Shop, After the Second Town Meeting

"Oh great," I thought to myself as my rag-tag crew trudged[33] up the hill behind me to my shop.

The mayor had stuck me with the "best and the brightest." A slacker, two kids, and some girl I've never even heard speak. I mean, I know they all meant well, but come on. How are

---

[33] to walk in an exhausted way

they supposed to fix my robot? I just needed space and more time, but nope, now I'm part of a team. I've never worked as part of a team. It's just not me.

I have to admit though, those waterproof wires I heard about could really help me out. And that coding idea isn't half bad. I still think that I don't need the other people, but their ideas are pretty good.

After reaching my garage, Xander was the first to run to my masterpiece. "So this is the robot we've heard so much about," said the unimpressed teenager.

"Hey," I snapped back. "It may not look pretty, but it's a darn good robot!"

"Except for the shorting out in water and the not doing what you want it to do," retorted[34] Xander.

"Guys, stop," Maiya said. "We're

---

[34] to reply in a harsh tone

getting distracted from what's important here. Can you please work together and get this done so our city can get back to normal?"

"Fine," I gave up. "Xander, do your thing. But I'll be watching you!"

Xander gave a fake salute and went to work, laying all the connectors he made out on the ground. One by one, he snapped his connectors on the ends of the wires, slowly making it waterproof, bit by bit. It was a slow and boring process because there were a lot of wires, but I had to hand it to the kid, he worked quickly with his invention. As unmotivated as Xander seems to be, he sure knows what he's doing.

"Done!" Xander announced, wiping the sweat away from his forehead. "That should be the last one. Let's test it out."

I carefully reached into the robot to press the power button. Everyone in the room, who had previously been bored out of their minds, now gave us their undivided attention. After seconds, it came to life, quietly humming with lights blinking.

"Okay," I said. "Let's not get too excited. Turning it on is only the first part. Now let's see if it can survive in the water."

With that I turned the robot so it was facing the water surrounding the garage and wound it up. With a jerk, the robot ran straight forward to the water.

With a loud splash, it rolled into the water and stopped after a few more seconds. Even though it was half-submerged, the robot reached into its container to grab the pipe-fixing parts, then started going through all the right motions to patch up a hole. I saw Maiya and Kelly nervously holding hands, and even I waited with bated breath [35]. Finally, the robot stopped moving, and we gathered around the finished product. It had worked!

Chapter 12
RUCHI

Mike's Mechanic Shop

There was excitement in the air in Mike's garage. Everyone was waiting for the final step, waiting for me. There was Mike himself, who built this robot from scratch in just a day; Xander, who somehow made electricity and water go together; and Kelly and Maiya, who united us for the good of everyone.

And there was me, Ruchi. The last puzzle piece to save the town.

Kelly spoke up. "So, Ruchi, it's all up to you now. The robot can move its arms and gears manually, but it needs to use its sensors so it can control itself underwater. We need your help." Xander and Mr. Mike pulled the robot out of the water and parked it in front of me.

I grabbed my laptop and a small green electronic device out of my bag. Everyone started crowding around me, and it felt different. I was used to working alone, but now I realize that it also feels good to work with other people. "I should do this more often," I thought to myself.

While the laptop was turning on, I looked at the robot in front of me. It seemed weird to think that this little machine that's shorter than I am could save an entire town. But the power of this little robot was far greater than anyone could imagine.

I connected the green device to the computer. "What is that?" Maiya asked curiously.

I held the device up so they could all see it better. "This is called a microcontroller. When I connect it to the sensors on the robot, it can read exactly what the sensors tell us, like how far away a break is in the wire or how close a wall is so we don't bump into it. Then, after reading the information, the robot uses the instructions I write with my program to do exactly what I want." I paused when my code lit up my computer screen.

"Whoa. Do you understand that?" Kelly asked in awe.

I nodded. "It really isn't that hard once you get the hang of it. It's just like reading and writing another language." I looked at Mike. "Just so we're all on the same page, you want me to detect the exact breaks in the pumps for patches, right?"

Mike nodded. "I can't risk going down there myself to position the robot, so you better not mess up," he grumbled. He pulled out a map of the pipe breaks from his back pocket. "If you want to make our life even easier, then tell the robot to follow this map to all the places the pumps have broken."

"On it," I said. My fingers were flying across the keyboard. The sound of tapping keys filled the garage. It sounded like one of those children's toys, a set of chattering teeth. I focused all my attention on the code on my laptop screen. It was crucial[36] that I didn't mess up now. Mistakes are okay to make when you're on your own, but when everyone is watching you, there's a lot more pressure to do

---

[36] extremely important

the best you can.

As if to answer my thoughts, Mike said, "Ruchi, don't worry if the code doesn't work the first time."

"Thanks. But, it's going to work just fine in the end."

When I had written about half the code, I disconnected the micro-controller from my own laptop and slowly hooked up the sensors and the other wires. My screen flashed as I pressed the button to send the code into the robot. There was a quiet beep, and I looked up. "So we have to pretend there's a pipe with a black break to test if the sensors work. Do you have anything that looks like a pipe?"

Xander quickly grabbed a long pipe from somewhere in the garage and drew a thick, black line down the middle. "Just hold it up, and the robot should go to it by itself and find the break," I instructed.

"You sure it won't cut my hands off, Ms. Brainiac?"

"No promises," I laughed, relieving the tension in the room. I typed in a quick command to turn on the microcontroller. There was another beep. The lights flashed, but nothing happened.

This was a problem.

"Um … let me go back to the code," I muttered.

"Sure. Take your time," Xander joked. "But remember, there's a whole town on the line here."

I scrolled up and down, carefully reading the code. I didn't dare blink in case I missed the error.

"There!" I said excitedly. "I forgot a closing tag, so the robot skipped a bunch of lines."

They all looked confused.

"Closing tags tell the machine where one line of code ends and another begins. It's kind of like putting a period at the end of a sentence," I explained.

"What's supposed to happen now?" Kelly asked.

"I only wrote half of it, just to test it. It's supposed to go up to the pump, move until it finds the break in the pipe, and then patch it up."

After I typed in the command again and heard the beep, the robot finally began to move by itself toward the makeshift pipe. We were all transfixed[37] as the robot slowly rolled up to the pipe and then shifted sideways. When it was in front of the black break, it stopped, then quickly used its arm to grab the patch from the container, then used the other arm to solder[38] and attach it to cover the

---

[37] to become motionless with wonder or amazement

[38] using heated metal to stick two things together

break.

"You did it!" Xander exclaimed, giving me a high-five.

"I'm not done yet ... I need to save a digital version of Mike's map to the microcontroller so the robot knows exactly where the breaks are. But after that we should be good to go!" After the first mistake, I wrote the code carefully. I felt ecstatic[39] seeing words on a screen actually bring something to life. This was what I had always dreamed of doing!

Sooner than I thought, I was finished. The mood in the garage was as eager as before. If anything, the excitement had grown tenfold.

This was it.

The final test of all our hard work over the last two days.

"I'm going to run a short test program. All the robot is going to do is

---

[39] extreme happiness

go to the location of the closest broken pump segment but stay above ground. That's going to test if the map works."

With one last beep, the robot whirred to life with LED [40] lights flickering on and off and arms shifting around. After a few moments of standing still, it took off into the street, moving in straight lines. "It's just following the pipelines," I reassured. After turning down two streets, it stopped suddenly and made loud beeping noises.

We all cheered loudly in the fading afternoon sun.

"We did it! The digital map works!" Kelly screamed with excitement.

Everything we worked on led up to this point: watching the robot do exactly what we had planned and finding the breaks in the pipe and following the map in its digital brain.

---

[40] a type of energy-saving light bulb

It was definitely worth all the planning and all the little road bumps along the way to see this magnificent sight. Now it's time for us to save Aaronville.

Chapter 13
KELLY

Mike's Mechanic Shop

Mike and Xander had put their differences aside for a little bit to add waterproof wiring to the robot, a fantastic start. But Ruchi was really the one that brought the robot to life with her programming. The way she worked with the code was like art—molding and shaping, cutting out and binding instructions as gracefully as a sculptor.

When we tested the robot again, it worked unbelievably well. We tested it outside of Mike's garage a little bit more before we called the mayor and the town council. While we were waiting for the council to come, we worked on making more patches for the pumps out of scrap metal and stuffing them all in the robot's containers. Maiya and I took a few breaks and just stood back to watch the scene. We were filled with pride and awe for our talented friends.

Ruchi nudged me.

"Well done, Kelly," she said. "And you too, Maiya."

"What are you talking about?" I said. "You, Xander, and Mr. Mike made this robot. The city is saved because of your talents!"

"Yeah, Ruchi," said Maiya. "You're the reason the robot is even functioning properly. No one else in Aaronville could have done it!"

"That may be true," said Ruchi. "But the three of us would have never gotten together if you guys didn't speak up. Without you two, I wouldn't have had the courage to work with others."

Before any of us could say another word, Mike announced the mayor was on her way. She was going to come any second, so we set up our robot to be ready for presenting.

~~~

After a super presentation of its abilities, the mayor quickly approved the robot. Mike and Xander were harnessing[41] it to the back of Mike's pickup truck while Ruchi went over the code. Again. And again.

"Ruchi, it is perfect," I said, as Maiya pulled her laptop away from her. "It's more than perfect. Don't

---

[41] combining straps, bands, and other parts to hold something in place

worry about it. Stop overworking it."

"But—" Ruchi stopped and took a deep breath. "Fine. Let's go do this."

Mike gave us two thumbs up and we all piled into the truck. We drove to Main Street with the mayor and unhooked our masterpiece. Some adults helped pull open the manhole covers leading to the pumps. We turned on the robot and carefully lowered it into the flooded pipelines.

"Once we fix these pipes, then all the water will get pumped out of the street and Aaronville will be normal again!" I said optimistically[42]. With some beeps and flashing lights, our robot rolled away to save the town. We didn't see any changes at first, but after a short time, Ruchi pointed something out.

"Look at the water!" she pointed at

---

[42] looking at situations with a positive attitude

a section of the street. Just a bit before, there was a large puddle covering it, but now, there was barely anything left, and water was seeping into the sewers normally.

Mayor Arscheene gave us a big smile. "Nice work, all of you. I have to admit, I had my doubts in the beginning. But this actually seems to be working quite well!"

"Mr. Mike, do you still have blueprints for the robot?" I asked, suddenly thinking of another idea.

"Of course, kid. Who do you think I am?"

"Just the best engineer ever. But I was thinking we could get this done even faster with more robots! Do you think we can build more?"

Mike snorted. "I only have two hands. How many more would I have to make?"

I turned around. Somehow, without us noticing, a large group of people had showed up on the sidewalks. They had been watching us put the robot into the pipeworks. Suddenly, a voice from the crowd shouted, "I can help!" Soon, more people joined in. "I can help too!" "And me!" "I'll make more parts if you need it!"

Amused, I looked back at Mike. "Will all these people be enough to make a few more robots?"

He sputtered[43] for a bit, speechless, and then nodded. "You've got spirit, kid." To the rest of the people, he roared, "Let's build some robots!"

"And connectors!" Xander added. "Yay for no electrocution!"

~~~

In three hours, a giant crowd of volunteers built three robots and thousands of connectors and parts. Considering everything was made

---

[43] to make a soft sound or mumble

from scratch, it was quite a feat[44].
When each robot was done, the
volunteers sent it underground to fix
the pumps. Slowly but surely, the
water vanished from the streets.
While Mr. Mike barked orders, Ruchi
came up to me.

"Now that is what I'm talking
about," said Ruchi. "You are as
responsible for this success as I am,
Kelly. Leading people and getting
them to work together takes skill, too.
Using other people's talents and
forming a team the way you did — it
was amazing. You and Maiya showed
everyone that kids are capable of
doing great things! Amazing job, you
guys!"

I was so overwhelmed by what
Ruchi said. All I could do was hug her.

~~~

With everyone's help, Aaronville

---

[44] an extraordinary act or achievement

was cleaned right before sunset. The town cheered when the final robot returned aboveground. It was incredible that the five of us were able to save the town with just our creativity and teamwork. It really doesn't take much to do amazing things: all you need is imagination, a strong desire to change the world, and courage to speak out and say, "I can help!"

Glossary

air of despair- a gloomy or sad environment

appreciative- feeling grateful

apprenticeship- a person who works for another in order to learn a certain skill

bated breath- holding your breath in anticipation

bounded- moved quickly

briskly- energetic and fast

clustered- standing close together

conduct- allows electricity to pass through it

considerate- showing care for another's feelings

countered- to be against something

displaced- moved or put out of the

usual or proper place

dutifully- doing something you are expected to do

ecstatic- extreme happiness

electrocution- to injure by electricity

empathy- being able to relate to how someone feels or thinks

enthusiastically- feeling eager or excited

erupted- to break out dramatically

feat- an extraordinary act or achievement

frantically- in a panic

gallivanting- to wander around

gulped- to eat quickly

harnessing- combining straps, bands, and other parts to hold something in place *inhabitable-* unable to be lived in

junctions- a point where two or more things are joined

LED- a type of energy-saving light bulb

mould- a waterproof mixture

nudged- to push gently to get someone's attention

optimistically- looking at situations with a positive attitude

programming- process of typing instructions in a special language so the computer can understand them

pseudocode- an outline of the code to make it easier to write

retorted- to reply in a harsh tone

solder- using heated metal to stick two things together

sparing- to hold back from harming or destroying

sputtered- to make a small sound or mumble

transfixed- to become motionless with wonder or amazement

triumphant- successful

trudged- to walk in an exhausted way

verge- to be close to

weave- to combine various elements to make a new whole

Discussion & Activities

Questions to Discuss as a Group:

1.) In the story, the townspeople had to work together to fix the broken pipes after the storm. Think about your life. Can you think of a time when you had to work together with other people to solve a problem? Do you think working together is better than working alone? Why?

2.) Mike is the mechanic who built the framework of the robot. At the beginning, do you think he cooperated well with the other people? Why or why not? How do you think Mike changed by the end of the book?

3.) Who is your favorite character from the book? Why? What are some characteristics you share with the character?

4.) Four jobs are presented in this book: mechanic, electrician, programmer, and leader. Which job interests you the most, and why? Which career would you want to learn more about?

5.) Each character in the book has personal flaws. Describe a conflict a character faced with himself or herself. How did he or she overcome these challenges?

6.) Think about the theme of this book. (There can be multiple answers!) How has this theme appeared throughout the book?

7.) In your opinion, what was the true success of the team? Was the success building a robot, or coming together and working as a team?

Activities:

1.) In Flooded, the citizens of Aaronville build a robot that is able to find the breaks in the pipe and fix them. If a storm destroyed your town, can you think of some ways to solve the problem? Draw out your design for a robot on a piece of paper. Let your creativity flow!

2.) Pretend you are a citizen of this town. Write a letter to Mayor Arscheene on how you would personally fix the problem.

3.) In your class, pick three other people you normally wouldn't work with. First, think of a problem in the world. It can be anything like ending world hunger or protecting endangered animals. Now, work with your group members to develop a solution to this problem. Think outside the box! Make sure to be open to everyone's opinions and ideas.

4.) Draw a picture of the town before and after the robot saved the day.

The Science Behind the Story

FIRST Things First

FIRST stands for For the Inspiration and Recognition of Science and Technology. This giant organization creates a game each year for teams of all grade levels to play. FIRST competitions aren't just your average basketball or football games. FIRST invites people with a love for innovation and engineering across the world to design and build robots and to compete with these robots in exciting new challenges against other robots. Robots can be built from Legos by elementary students or from sheet metal and electrical wires by high school students. The creators of FIRST, Woodie Flowers and Dean Kamen, wanted to showcase the creativity and imagination of kids everywhere and to inspire children to go into science or technology fields when they grow up.

FIRST has four divisions: FIRST Robotics Competition (FRC), for high school students; FIRST Tech Challenge (FTC), for middle and high school students; FIRST Lego League (FLL), for middle school students; and Junior FIRST Lego League (Jr. FLL), for elementary school students. These divisions all have challenges that change each year. Students in these four divisions compete at the local level. If a state has enough teams, winners advance to the state championship and from there, to the international FIRST Championship, which has taken place in St. Louis, Missouri for the last five years. These challenges are different for each division. For example, in 2014, the game for FRC was Aerial Assist, where robots had to score points by throwing exercise balls into goal zones, while the game for FLL in 2014 was World Class, where the activities had to deal with different, innovative approaches to learning new things. To find out more information, go to www.usfirst.org.

ThunderChickens: Our Team in an Eggshell

This book was written by members of the robotics team 217, ThunderChickens. We are a group of high school students from the Utica Community Schools district in Macomb County, Michigan who compete in the FIRST Robotics Competition (FRC) league. The ThunderChickens were founded more than ten years ago. We won the international FRC Championship in

2006 and 2008. Today, our team has grown to include more than fifty students and more than ten mentors.

In just six weeks, starting in January, we build large robots that are three to four feet tall and weigh more than 100 pounds. We work out of the Van Dyke Ford Plant in Sterling Heights, Michigan. Ford Motor Company is one of our biggest sponsors. Each of our students is a part of one or more departments on the team, including design, mechanical, electrical, programming, public relations, and competition strategy. No previous experience is necessary to join our team— for most students, it is a major learning experience. If the characters in the book were on our team, Mike would be a mechanical mentor, Ruchi would be a programming student, Xander would be an electrical student, and Maiya and Kelly would be public relations students.

In addition to building a robot, we host many events for students in our community. In the past, we've been a part of charity and volunteer events, including Give Kids a Smile, the General Motors Diabetes Walk, cleaning up our local river, and making fleece blankets for children in hospitals. Most importantly, we host outreach events involving science, technology, engineering, and mathematics (STEM). They are open to all students, from elementary school kids to high school teenagers. So far, we've hosted two Robot Days, educational events where we show off

 the robots we've made in the past as well introduce the different departments of our team. We hosted Robot Day at our public library, where we taught kids how to rivet and drill (mechanical), connect the wiring of a robot (electrical), code (programming), and 3D print parts (design). More than 300 students came to explore engineering.

In addition to Robot Days, we've also hosted Thunderquest, the biggest FLL qualifying tournament in Michigan, for the past six years. During the 2014 Thunderquest competition, 55 teams and hundreds of students competed.

Stars of the Robotics World

This is a list of some influential people in the field of robotics. These people are inventors and engineers, but most of all, they are innovators of new ways to change the world.

Dean Kamen, one of the founders of the FIRST Robotics organization, is the inventor of the Segway and holds numerous other patents as well. He founded FIRST in 1989.

Woodie Flowers is another founder of the FIRST Robotics organization. He received his doctorate degree at the Massachusetts Institute of Technology.

Grace Hopper was one of the first programmers ever. Also known as "Amazing Grace," she coded on the Harvard Mark I computer, one of the first computers created.

Henry Ford was best-known for being the founder of the Ford Motor Company. He was the first to use the assembly line effectively to mass produce Model Ts for the public.

Ruchi Sanghvi was one of the first female engineers at Facebook and Dropbox. Currently, there's a big gender gap in the computer science industry, meaning there are many more men than women in the field.

More Than Fiction

Even though this story is fictional, there have been many examples of people using engineering and computer science to solve problems caused by natural disasters. In 2013, after a tornado in Oklahoma, a tech company called Palantir used different engineering methods to connect emergency responders with the victims. This includes a mobile app with information about damage assessment, a Web form for better communications between the volunteers and the citizens, and a computer network for intensive data analysis.

However, kids have amazing ideas for disaster relief too! During one of our Robot Days, we asked the students come up with different ideas for helping the town get rid of its flooding. Here are some of the great solutions they engineered:

Jaydin Shick, 2nd Grade

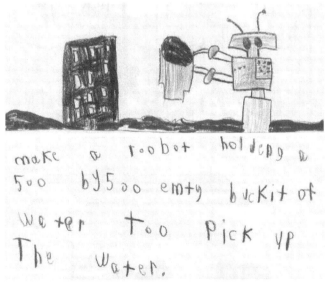

make a roobot holdcng a 500 by500 emty bvckit of wa ter too pick vp The water.

Rory Donnelly, *4th Grade*

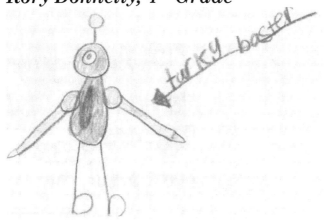

turky baster

Jacob Schick, *6th Grade*

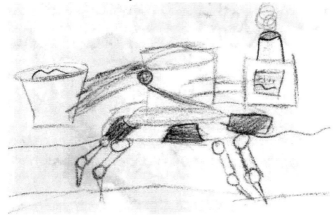

Anthony Greco, 7th Grade

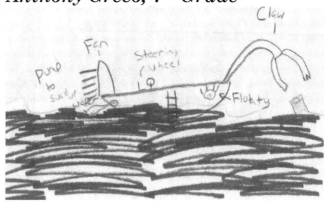

Corey Reynolds, 8th Grade

"Move the city away from the flood with the rocket boosters."

Acknowledgements

This book would not have been possible without all of the input and support of FRC Team 217, the ThunderChickens. Special thanks to the students on the team: Jacob Bely, Victor Buzgan, Sean Castle, Grace Ciaramella, Hayden Chase, Evan de Jesus, Steven Dubey, Dylan Gaines, Derek Gee, Cameron Gudobba, Ryan Henigan, Hannah Imboden, Zachary Komondy, Vincent LaRocca, Sidney Leming, Christina Li, Kevin Li, Jason Li, Joseph McMullen, Adam McNeil, Adam Misch, Parker Misch, Calvin Montgomery, Mary Najjar, Vanessa Najjar, Erica Nanni, Sowmyaw Nakkina, Vivian Nguyen, Devon Ochenski, Aakash Patel, Alouk Patel, Kush Patel, Dylan Plummer, Emily Poirier, Manvir Sandhu, Darpan Shah, Nygel Sejismundo, Kenneth Shivers, Jacob Smellie, Drew Stauffer,

Stephen Stockman, Reece Troia, Aditya Vageesh, Giulio Vario, Matthew Vogt, Preya Vyas, Bailey Whitehead, Carina Willcock, and Grant Zuccaro.

No robotics team would be complete without amazing mentors, and the ThunderChickens are no exception. Many professionals have joined our ranks over the years, including Kyle Abbott, Ronald Arscheene, Michael Attan, Bill Baedke, Don Bartlett, Mike Beem, Paul and Alexandra Doan, Jeff and Julie Kausch, Bob and Rose Korson, Kelly Kozlowski, Kevin Kutscher, Deborah McNeil, Ian Milne, Tony Moraccini, Justin Schultz, Donavon Whitehead, Siobhan Whitehead, Aaron Willcock, Gary Yahr, and Jim Yaxley.

Many of our mentors served as inspiration for our characters in the book. Ronald Arscheene is the head mentor of our team who's been with us since the very start. Mr. Arscheene is always able to pull us together, even when things get crazy with building the robot. He inspires us before every competition to succeed and pushes us to achieve our potential.

Another one of our major inspirations was Kelly Kozlowski, the public relations (PR) and marketing mentor for our team. During every competition, our PR department writes newsletters (The Thunder Press) about the people and teams of FIRST. Kelly always encourages us to aim higher, think bigger, and never think anything is out of our reach. She never says no. Without her support when we initially brainstormed the book, it never would have become a reality.

The programming mentor on our team, Aaron Willcock, was on ThunderChickens when he was in high school. After graduating, he returned to teach software to the new students. Even though he is a full time student and has a job, he is committed to inspiring and teaching the team. During competitions, he not only makes sure our robot is functioning, but is constantly helping other teams. He inspires the entire team to keep fighting and is our model of gracious professionalism, which is the idea of helping others even when you're competing against them.

At the beginning of this project, children's book author Kelly DiPucchio provided us a lot of advice on how and where to start, and the direction to take our publishing.

Thank you again to everyone who contributed to the writing of this book.

~Special Note to Kyle Abbott~

The name of the elementary school, Abbott Elementary, was inspired by Kyle Abbott, one of our biggest supporters. She was there from the very beginning, when we came up with the idea of writing a book and encouraged people to share their unique talents. Kyle was not only instrumental in the writing and editing processes, but also with the publishing steps to bring this book to life. She kept us, the authors, motivated even when nothing seemed to work out.

Our relationship with Kyle began when we approached the Abrams Foundation for a team sponsorship. Kyle is the Abrams Foundation board president and she took a deep interest in our team. The foundation has been supporting us for six years. Their support allows us to help other robotics teams. They have also given grants that provided the means for two of our teachers to attend a national STEM conference and to publish this book.

Over the past couple years, Kyle has been a source of immeasurable assistance and inspiration. Her enthusiasm for robotics and STEM is infectious. When we all got writer's block (at the same time), she pushed us through it with encouragement. When we were overwhelmed with school, she got us back on track.

Kyle attends as many of our competitions as she can. She even attended the Buckeye Regional in Cleveland last year and cheered as hard as we did when we won the Chairman's Award, which is given to the team that best reflects the pillars of FIRST. She knew how hard we had worked and was just as proud as any other member of the team.

Kyle is not just our sponsor; she is also a mentor and a friend. We are infinitely grateful for all that she has done for the team and all the time she has given. Thank you, Kyle.

Made in the USA
Middletown, DE
19 March 2015